LONG WEEKEND IN THE SHOW

A SLIGHTLY SCARY SHORT STORY

ALEXANDRIA BLAELOCK

BlueMere Books
MELBOURNE, AUSTRALIA

Publisher's Note: This is a work of fiction. Names, characters, places, and incidents are a product of the author's imagination. Locations and public names are sometimes used for atmospheric purposes. Any resemblance to actual people, living or dead, or to businesses, companies, events, institutions, or locations is completely coincidental.

Copyright © 2020 Alexandria Blaelock.

All rights reserved. No part of this publication may be reproduced, distributed or transmitted in any form or by any means, including photocopying, recording, or other electronic or mechanical methods, without the prior written permission of the publisher, except in the case of brief quotations embodied in critical reviews and certain other non-commercial uses permitted by copyright law.

For permission requests, please contact enquiries@bluemerebooks.com.

Ordering Information:
Discounts are available on quantity purchases. For details, contact orders@bluemerebooks.com.

Phoenix Child/Alexandria Blaelock
paperback ISBN: 978-1-925749-06-9
digital ISBN: 978-1-925749-07-6

Book Layout © BookDesignTemplates.com

LONG WEEKEND
IN THE SNOW

Jennifer's sigh fell as quietly as the snow falling outside the window.

"Snow again" she muttered, though there was no one to hear.

Even when it didn't snow, it snowed! It felt like there had never been a season other than winter.

"What I wouldn't give for a tropical beach holiday, and a sun-warmed Mai Tai," she told the evening gloom.

Still no sign of Justin - what was taking him so long? Was he lost?

The heavy clouds creeping across the sky made the tree shadows waver, the snowman seemed to be waving at her.

Perhaps calling her out to play, or signalling a warning.

Shivering reflexively, she pulled her cardigan tighter around her body. Then pulled her socks up for good measure.

The sullen red glow of the banked fire lured her over, and she inhaled the soft, warm smell of smoke as she bent to warm her hands.

Ideally, she'd have it stoked and roaring, but the earthquakes had been bad recently, and she couldn't risk it.

Not to mention that Justin had been gone for days and the wood heap was almost as low as the food stocks.

Even though the snow was as deep as the window sills, perhaps it was time to forage for wood. She'd managed the keep the path mostly clear despite the post-quake flurries, but it was still an effort to walk.

Maybe Justin had fallen or lost the path. Should she go look for him?

Perhaps, after a cold clear night, it would be sufficiently frozen to walk across.

Jennifer had no idea, she was a City girl who knew nothing about life in the country, let alone halfway up a mountain.

Not that it mattered, the night was drawing in, and there was nothing she could do until morning.

She grabbed the last crust of bread from the pantry on her way back to bed.

When had the power gone out? Was it Tuesday?

Not for the first time, Jennifer wished she was one of those super organised people whose phones and laptops were always charged.

Stranded in this tiny, if beautiful cottage with no knowledge of what was going on back home was torture.

And without power, there was nothing to do but sit in silence with her thoughts. And she'd almost used all of them up.

Thinking wasn't that much fun anyway.

And whose idea had it been to take a trip to the mountains?

Justin's.

After that massive argument when she'd called it quits, he'd suggested a long weekend at Mount Moira, just the two of them.

At the time, she'd thought it was an attempt to make amends, a bid for reconciliation.

How had he described it?

She couldn't remember.

Was it possible he'd meant to leave her here alone all along?

Poor sweet Justin? Surely not.

Yet he'd taken the car and left her there.

"Shopping for supplies," he said as he drove away. Never to be seen again.

Well, never say never.

She sighed again and pulled the bed covers more tightly around her.

Such a shame they couldn't bring her black Labrador, his warmth would be handy about now.

Though Ninja had never really taken to Justin.

She'd thought the dog was just jealous but had Ninja been trying to tell her something with his hostility?

She'd trusted the dog's judgement on so much else, why not Justin?

The tremors startled her awake. They increased in intensity, and she was thrown from the bed as if by a vengeful hand.

Mugs, plates and books pelted down around her as she scrambled under the bed for safety.

She was grimly amused that so much of it was unbreakable melamine.

While the cottage owners weren't advertising this as an earthquake zone on Airbnb, they'd clearly put some thought into minimising their on costs.

Actually, why hadn't they sent anyone to clean cottage seeing as they should have left by now?

Justin had told her a long weekend, and he was a bit tight where money was concerned, so it didn't seem likely he'd booked more than three nights.

His miserliness had been the cause of more than one disagreement, and a significant point of difference in their outlook.

It was a big part of her decision to break up with him.

Though of course with the earthquakes and snowstorms, maybe the owners couldn't get through either.

Could the storms be blocking both them and Justin?

As the tremors faded away, Jennifer resolved to never again leave home without an emergency coffee supply. And nuts, crackers or some other kind of sustaining snack. And a small torch. Maybe a deck of cards. Definitely a notebook and pen.

Of all the "essentials" she was carrying in her enormous tote bag, only the tissues had been useful, and there weren't enough of them to deal with the cold weather nose drip.

Lucky the cottage came with too many tea towels, though they weren't very kind to her face.

At least her clothes were more or less appropriate, so she was more or less warm. Somewhat warmer when she wore the bedding too.

She'd been expecting a ski lodge, not a cosy cottage.

Why can't men communicate more clearly, she wondered.

Why not say "I've hardly seen you these last few months, so I've booked us a cottage in the mountains where we can get naked and catch up." Instead of "Let's go into the hills for lunch."

That lunch seemed so long ago.

They'd visited a cosy French cafe and eaten a delicious Cassoulet with buttery garlic mashed potato and green beans, followed by spiced apple Tarte Tatin, and rather too much wine.

Then they'd taken a walk around the wood fire scented village to help it settle.

There'd been a little window shopping before Justin insisted they go into the mystical shop and have their fortunes told.

He'd disappeared behind a curtain while an older woman wearing heavy eyeliner, jangly bangles and a headscarf took her behind another.

She'd smiled when she saw the cool dark room was exactly as she expected - dim and partially lit by candles with bunches of herbs and other weird things hanging from the rafters.

Jars and bottles were arranged on shelves, but the room was dominated by a small table in the centre on which rested a large, clear crystal ball in a silver stand.

It was a bit over the top.

She guessed her fortune would include something about a tall, blond and handsome man (conveniently like Justin), as well as overseas travel and a long, happy life.

The smooth hypnotic tone of the woman's soft, deep and husky voice, punctuated by rhythmic bangle shaking and the heavy scent of incense were shutting down her logical brain.

Without considering whether it was wise or safe, she surrendered to the illusion.

Taking a seat across from the old woman, Jennifer accepted a bitingly cold and bitter drink and took a sip.

The old woman took Jennifer's left hand, held it palm up in her warm, soft, grip, and gazed intently into the ball.

"You are deeply loved...

"You are successful at everything you turn your hand to...

"You have a promising future...

"But first will come a period of great suffering...

"Your path will be cold and dark...

"You are in great danger...

"I wish I could do something to help you."

Well, ahem.

As far as fortunes go, Jennifer thought, this one sucked. She tried to rouse herself, get off the chair, and out of the room but just fell on the floor.

She'd tried to crawl away, but everything went dark.

And she woke up here in the cottage.

Crawling out from under the bed, she tried to remember the drive to the mountains.

And if she had even seen Justin in the cottage.

Had he really been there, or did she dream he told her he was getting supplies?

She was starting to worry more about being alone and inadequately prepared in a strange place than being cold and hungry.

It was as if foreboding was a fog rising from the floorboards.

She ran to the bathroom and threw up the stale bread crust. Resting her head on the toilet seat, as she recovered, she tried to work out what it was she was missing.

What about this situation wasn't right?

Aside from everything.

She got off the floor and went to the sink. After swilling some cold water around her mouth, she took a longer drink that somehow echoed the taste of the fortune teller's offering.

She splashed cold water on her face, and as she looked down at the sink, she noticed something. Or rather, didn't notice something.

Her toiletries were here, but there were no signs of Justin's.

The blood drained from her face, she felt cold and a bit dizzy with the shock.

Spinning around, she looked for evidence of him, but there was one towel, one toothbrush, one deodorant.

No shaving cream, no razor, no aftershave.

Sobbing, she lurched into the main room and ripped open the cupboards hauling everything out onto the floor. Then emptied all the drawers, pulled everything off the shelves, and kicked the contents around the floor.

No bags, no clothes, no nothing.

Nothing to suggest he'd been in the cottage.

How was that possible?

Leaving the mess where it was, she opened the cottage door and walked out into the snow.

The cold wetness brought her to her senses, and she paused at the start of the path.

What was she doing walking out into the show with no shoes or coat?

What did she hope to achieve?

Shrugging, she ignored the cold, and her logical brain, and fought her way down the path to the gate.

She noticed that despite all the upheaval, there was no earthquake evidence in the garden.

No leaf litter, no fallen branches, no dirty messed up snow. It was clean, level and white.

Not only that, but there were no bird or animal sounds - the forest was deathly quiet.

And weirdly, the air smelled and tasted stale, not like fresh mountain air at all.

Was it her imagination, or was it slightly warmer outside than in the cottage?

Her skin crawled, and she turned to look at the snowman. It was in one piece and appeared to be studying her intently.

She turned back and oddly conscious of the snowman, reached out to open the gate.

The wood was smooth in her hand, and the hinges creaked as she pulled the gate towards her and took a small step through.

And then another.

And another.

And yelped as she stepped into an invisible barrier.

Reaching out with both hands, she found that it stretched from the ground, higher than she could reach.

Her skin was crawling with more than the cold as she kept one hand on the barrier, turned to her right and started walking to see how far it extended.

Past the snowman, through the forest, and in a very short time back to the path.

She barely felt the cold any longer.

As if it would make a difference, she turned and walked back the way she came, this time trying to see through the barrier.

Back once more at the path, it seemed there was something out there. A strange discolouration in the sky, like an aurora, but different. It seemed to be coming closer, impossibly fast.

Jennifer ducked instinctively and crouched looking up in terror.

It wasn't an aurora or any other kind of astronomical event.

It was Justin's face floating impossibly large in the sky outside the barrier.

An enormous hand reached out, and the earth rocked as it moved closer to Justin's face.

His eyes lit up when he saw her, and he smiled.

His smile became a grin as she was rocked by the increasing earthquake intensity.

And she realised she wasn't here for a long weekend in the snow, she was imprisoned in a snow globe.

THE END

ABOUT THE AUTHOR

Alexandria Blaelock writes stories, some of them for *Ellery Queen's Mystery Magazine* and *Pulphouse Fiction Magazine*. She's also written four self-help books applying business techniques to personal matters like getting dressed, cleaning house, and feeding your friends.

As a recovering Project Manager, she's probably too fond of sticking to plan. She lives in a forest because she enjoys birdsong, the scent of gum leaves and the sun on her face. When not telecommuting to parallel universes from her Melbourne based imagination, she watches K-dramas, talks to animals, and drinks Campari. At the same time.

Discover more at www.alexandriablaelock.com.

OTHER SHORT STORIES BY ALEXANDRIA BLAELOCK

Kiss of Death
Long Weekend in the Snow
Shining Star
Phoenix Child
Ship in a Bottle
Lady of the Looking Glass
Simone Says Hands in the Air
Life in the Security Directorate
Fate in Your Hands
Love in the Security Directorate
Alma's Grace
Payton's Run
The Guardian's Vigil
The Life and Death of Carmelita Basingstoke
Balancing the Book

BOOKS BY ALEXANDRIA BLAELOCK

Stress Free Dinner Parties
Build Your Signature Wardrobe
Holistic Personal Finance
Ms Blaelock's Book of Minimally Viable
Housekeeping

www.ingramcontent.com/pod-product-compliance
Lightning Source LLC
Chambersburg PA
CBHW070543190726
48291CB00016B/1780